"Jeepers!" Daphne exclaimed. "Look where we are — London, England! It's lucky Scooby won five train tickets across Europe."

"Only Scooby could win first prize for eating the most Scooby Snacks," said Fred.

"All aboard the European Express!" cried the train's owner, Roger Railton. "Welcome to the final run of my grandfather's famous rail line."

SCOOBY-DOO!

Scooby-Doo AND THE International Express

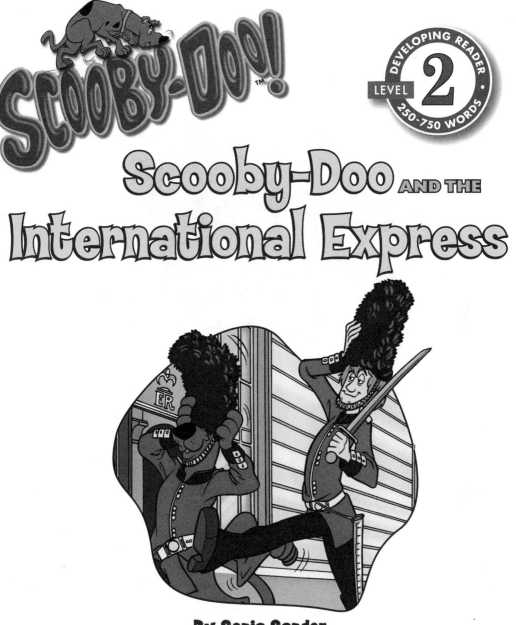

By Sonia Sander
Illustrated by Duendes del Sur

WORLDWIDE PUBLISHING

SCHOLASTIC INC.
New York Toronto London Auckland
Sydney Mexico City New Delhi Hong Kong

ISBN-13: 938-0-545-16283-8
ISBN-10: 0-545-16283-1

Designed by Michael Massen

12 11 10 9 8 7 6 5 4 3 2 1   9 10 11 12 13 14/0

Printed in the U.S.A.
First printing, September, 2009

"Why is this the train's final run?" asked Velma. "I'll tell you as soon as we're onboard the train, Velma," said Roger. "That's my rival, Sam Snitch. I don't want him to hear the story."

Roger invited the gang to join him in his office, which was a special car on the train.

"My grandfather worried he would run out of money. One day he hid his entire fortune," he told them.

"The only clue he left behind was this old deck of cards and this broken clock. Now we need money to fix the train, but we can't find it."

"Jinkies!" said Velma. "I can't believe no one noticed all the queens were missing from the card deck."

"Buckingham Palace is the only place to look for a queen when you're in London," said Fred.

Daphne turned to Shaggy and Scooby. "Stop fooling around, you two! We need your help!"

But — ruh-roh — it was too late! Shaggy and Scooby tumbled into the guard house.

"Like, hold on, Scoob!" cried Shaggy. They had broken through a secret wall.

"Jinkies!" said Velma. "It's another clue! This note says, Leonardo da Vinci's famous smile."

Roger was thrilled that Scooby and the gang had found a clue.

But not everyone was happy about it.

"Zoinks!" cried Shaggy. "Like, don't look now, but a spooky ghost is after us!"

Scooby and Shaggy escaped from the ghost. They were very happy to get off the train in Paris. Their first stop was the Louvre, a famous art museum.

"Like, I sure am glad to be off that creepy train. Hold still, Scoob," said Shaggy. He pretended to paint his buddy's picture.
Scooby tried to stand still, but he tripped and knocked the *Mona Lisa* off the wall!

Luckily, Fred was there to catch the painting. But not before a slip of paper flew out of the frame.

Velma picked it up. "You'll need a red scarf and your running shoes," she read.

"It sounds like we're going to run with the bulls," said Fred. "Next stop, Spain!"

Back on the train, the gang shared their find with Roger.

Before they could celebrate, the train went dark.

A spooky warning from the ghost appeared.

"Like, if that ghost is so unhappy," gulped Shaggy, "maybe we should stop looking."

19

The rest of the gang wouldn't let Shaggy give up.

When the train arrived in Spain, the gang joined the crowd running from the bulls.

"Like, the only clue I want to find here is a safe place to hide!" cried Shaggy.

"Look!" cried Fred. "Come on, gang, we're almost at the finish line."

As soon as the race was over, Shaggy and Scooby fell to the ground.

"Like, next time let's skip to the end and forget the race," panted Shaggy.

"I'm with you, Shaggy," said Daphne. She leaned on a big bull statue.

"Jeepers! I think I just found the fourth clue!" she cried.

Velma grabbed it. "Venice, here we come!"

Scooby and the gang almost didn't make it to Venice.

Late that night, the ghost tried to stop them again. He unhitched the last train car. It raced back down the track.

But thanks to Scooby and Shaggy's hard work, the gang made it back to the train.

"Like, this is the longest train ride ever!" said Shaggy. "I'm pooped, Scoob!"

"Re, roo," Scooby agreed.

When the train arrived in Venice, the gang headed to the Grand Canal.

"The next clue must be hidden under the famous Bridge of Sighs," said Velma.

"Everyone knows about the bridge's promise of true love sealed by a kiss," said Daphne.

"And about the prisoners that were held inside it," Fred added.

Splash! Scooby and Shaggy ended up in the canal.

But not before they found the last clue in a crack in the bridge.

"Time doesn't stop!" read Velma. "Roger's grandfather clock!"

"The gold must be hidden inside," said Fred. "Let's go, gang!"

With the ghost on their heels, Scooby and the gang raced back to the train.

Daphne quickly set the hands of the clock to the correct time.

A tick and a tock later, gold burst out.

Fred ripped off the ghost's mask. "I had a feeling Roger's rival was behind this!"

"If it weren't for you meddling kids, I would be the only train line in Europe," said Sam Snitch.

"Like, this dinner from Roger was the best thanks ever," said Shaggy.

"Rummy, rummy," Scooby agreed. "Scooby-Dooby-Doo!"